Rook
Anthony McGowan

First published in 2017 in Great Britain by
Barrington Stoke Ltd
18 Walker Street, Edinburgh, EH3 7LP

www.barringtonstoke.co.uk

A CIP catalogue record for this book is available from the British Library upon request

ISBN: 978-1-78112-723-0

Printed in China by Leo

This book has dyslexia-friendly features

For Phil Earle: friend and inspiration

One

It was a day of hard graft. The fields sparkled with frost, which delighted his dark eye. But the hard crust meant that he had to peck and scratch to get at the worms and grubs lurking in the cold earth below.

But he was happy.

Happy because he was with his mob, a loose flock of rooks and jackdaws, his brothers, his sisters, his friends.

Happy because the wide fields and woods and sky belonged to him.

Happy because he was young in his world, and had tasted little of pain and hunger in the six months since he had first hopped from the nest of twigs and stretched his black wings.

The rooks squawked and the jackdaws chattered and clacked as they plodded up and down the furrows. The light was failing, and soon they'd fly off together in a ragged cloud to roost for the night.

Earlier that day they'd had some sport with a male sparrowhawk. A gang of them surrounded the raptor in a copse of oak and willow and their harsh cries rang like laughter as they poured scorn on it. The sparrowhawk was smaller than the rooks, about the same size as the jackdaws. Under the blue-grey of its back and wings, there was a creamy breast, with black bars, but also a blush of orange, the colour of an autumn sunset.

Pretty or not, the mob hated it, and drove it deeper into the trees. Then they became bored with their game and went back to the endless search for food.

But, oddly, the sparrowhawk had appeared again later. He watched them from the naked branches at the top of an ash tree. This time they ignored him.

And yet, somewhere in the back of the rook's mind was a twisting worm of doubt, a shadow on his mind.

And, if he had seen it, a shadow on the ground ...

As the rook pecked and scratched and worried, he sensed that the flock was ready to fly.

But this wasn't the usual lazy flurry, with stragglers still pulling at worms as the leaders flew off. This time there was a sudden electric energy. And then the cries came, the shrieks of terror.

Now the rook caught the fear, opened his wings and sprang into the air. One beat, two. The earth was three metres below him, and the safety of the trees only a few seconds away.

And then a force hit him, like nothing he had ever felt before. It seemed to melt his bones and turn his flesh to vapour. And in the bone-crushing impact there was a sharper pain, searing into him like hot needles.

The hit took the rook down, and he felt the frosted earth rise up to crush his face and breast.

And then, jab, jab, two more stabs of agony. And he knew. He had been taken. He had made the great change, from hunter to hunted, from eater to eaten. He felt the claws dig deeper into his back, felt the curved beak gouge into his flesh, felt meat – his own meat, the meat of him – being torn away.

But rooks are never an easy meal. He flapped wildly with his wings, trying to shake off the predator on his back. He reached around to find something he could peck at with his own strong beak, and pecked only at air.

But he saw.

Not, as he'd thought, the dark and pretty male sparrowhawk. This was a pale brown female. She was much larger and more powerful than her mate – a killer of pigeons and magpies, not sparrows. Even so, he knew it was rare for her to take on something as big as a rook.

But she had done it, and now she was relentless. She stabbed again with her hooked beak, like an artist painting with a fine brush. And what she painted was death.

The rook twisted in agony, and she let go with one set of talons, so she could get a better grip. The talons were her killing tools, and she needed a soft place to insert them, a chink under the skull where she could pierce the brain, or a narrow gap between the ribs, where she could feel for his frantic heart.

But now the rook had a split second of release and the chance to turn to face her. Now he could see where to stab his own beak. He managed to reach the hawk's breast feathers, but he drew no blood.

And now both her sets of claws were on him again, in him, slicing into the flesh of his breast.

She opened her wings around him, like a tent, as if to hide the final horror. Because, yes, she would eat him while he still lived. He would watch her pluck the short feathers on his breast, tear out strips of dark flesh, throw back her head and swallow ...

NO!

He had fight in him yet. He kicked out, strong. His talons were not razor-sharp like hers, but they were tough as iron, and they scratched and raked at her. And at last he landed a good hard peck in the face of the hawk, which made her pull back, and flap her wings. But still, two talons were locked in the breast of the rook. She screeched, and aimed two savage pecks at the rook's eyes.

He knew he only had one last effort in him, one last chance. He kicked again, and pecked, and it was enough to loosen her grip. With a frenzied flapping, he broke away and took to the air.

He was too weak, too hurt – he skimmed just above the frozen field. But he was free. He was alive.

And then it came again, the thud of the hawk's dive. Somehow she had overtaken him, and fallen on him again from above. He wanted to live, but so did she, and to live meant to kill.

The hawk and the rook crashed to the ground. The sparrowhawk stooped to pull out a beakful of his breast feathers. The pain of it only made the rook utter a last, feeble croak.

The rook was in shock now with this horror, with this pain. His eyes grew dark, but beyond the darkness he sensed a light. He began to lift up into the sky, above the canopy of the trees, and he imagined himself soaring up for ever into the golden evening.

Then there was a noise. A noise that would usually send him and the flock flapping into the sky. A noise that shouldn't have brought hope, but danger.

The excited barking of a dog.

Two

My dad was on night shift and he wanted a sleep,
so me and Kenny took Tina out for a walk so her
yapping didn't keep him awake. Tina wasn't one
of those clever dogs that can do tricks, unless you
count eating socks as a trick. But she loved me and
Kenny – Kenny most of all – because we'd saved her
when some bad kids hurt her and left her for dead.

Tina's favourite walk was over the fields past
the church. The church was on a hill and you could
see for ever, down across the flat fields and little
woods. My dad told us that when he was a kid
they'd sometimes find human bones from the really
old graves on the side of the hill, and then they'd
chase each other with an arm bone or a leg bone.
Behind the church there were big flat graves like
stone coffins and some of them had broken tops,

and our dad said it was a big dare to climb inside one, and lie with the bones.

We didn't completely believe him, but the graveyard was a creepy place at night, and we always hurried back from a walk so we didn't get caught there when the ghosts came out and skeletons chased you, and vampires rose up from their graves to bite you.

I let Tina off her lead when we were away from the road, and she ran around like mad weeing on everything, like she'd been holding it in for a week.

"How much money would you get in one of the graves for?" Kenny said.

"How long would I have to be in there?" I asked.

"For a whole night, not just in and out like a bath."

Kenny hated baths, and always jumped out before he was even wet.

"I don't know," I said.

"A million pounds?"

"Probably," I said. "There's a lot you can do with a million pounds. Dad wouldn't have to work nights and we could buy a car, and we could go to visit Mum ..."

Our mum had left home when me and Kenny were small. Kenny had learning difficulties.

Sometimes he could see things really clearly, maybe because there wasn't as much stuff in the way, like there is with other people. But when he was little it was hard for my mum, and my dad wasn't great. Then, after years of nothing, my mum got in touch a while back, which was weird, but OK. She lived in Canada, and wanted us to come and stay with her for the holidays.

"So," Kenny went on, "would you do it for half a million?"

"Yeah," I said. "I would."

Kenny thought for a bit. He had a stick, so he could whip at any weed stupid enough to poke its head up.

"Would you do it for a tenner?" he asked.

"No."

Kenny nodded. He liked to know things for sure. He wanted to know exactly how much it'd take for me to sleep in a cold grave with old bones.

"For twenty thousand?"

"Er, yeah, probably."

"Two thousand?"

"No."

"Seven thousand?"

"Yeah, if the Queen came and handed me the cash on a silver tray."

That made Kenny laugh. I could see by his face that he was imagining the Queen coming to our house in her Rolls Royce and giving me the money.

"What about you?" I asked. "Would you do it for a million pounds?"

Kenny shook his head, like a wasp was attacking him. "NO WAY!"

"What would you do it for, then?"

"NOTHING!"

I'd been waiting for that.

"Hah, got you!" I said. "You said you'd sleep in a grave for nothing. And when you say something, it says in the Bible that that's as good as a promise, and if you've promised you've got to do it."

Kenny looked appalled. He would rather break his arm than break a promise. But I couldn't keep a straight face, and we both started to laugh. He jumped on me, which made Tina bark like mad, and then we ran down out of the dark of the trees and into the bare fields beyond.

The three of us stopped, dead, and stared. You couldn't miss it, but it was also impossible to work out what was going on. There was a bundle of feathers, a flurry of movement, a screeching noise.

Tina was the first to react. She tore across the frosty ground towards the action, barking as she ran.

"It's birds fighting!" Kenny said. "Catch Tina, or she might ..."

I chased after Tina. It was the most exciting thing that had ever happened to her. She always used to jump after birds in the garden, and even she must have known it was hopeless. But now she had a chance.

I looked again at the ball of feathers. A hawk had got a crow. It was a right old battle. But it was a battle that Tina was going to finish if she reached them.

"Stay, Tina," I yelled. "Come here, girl, you stupid dog!"

But it was no use. She was almost on them.

The hawk looked like it had been getting the better of the crow, but just as Tina was about to dive in, it gave an angry screech and flapped up and away. Tina couldn't resist the target, and she leaped up to try to catch it in mid-air. A dog with bigger legs might have done it, but Tina was a Jack Russell, with stupid little legs. Even so, it wasn't a bad effort. Her jaws snapped shut millimetres from the hawk's long tail.

But all Tina's effort went into the jump, and none into the landing. She did a half-turn in the air and landed on her arse, which was kind of funny. It also saved the life of the injured crow. If she'd landed on her feet she'd have gone straight for the bird on the ground, and made a dog's dinner of it. But her rubbish fall gave me just enough time to grab her collar and click her lead on.

Tina went mental, barking and snapping at the crow. Kenny ran up and I gave the lead to him, while I looked at the bird.

I thought it was dead, for a second. The only movement was the wind ruffling its feathers.

"Is it alive?" Kenny said. He was still holding Tina back.

"I don't know."

"Pick it up and see," he said.

I didn't really want to. The thought of touching it if it was dead gave me the creeps. I remembered something about fleas and lice on dead animals, and it made me itchy just thinking about it. And if it was only stunned, then that beak looked like it could do some damage.

"Here," Kenny said, "you hold Tina."

He thrust the lead back into my hand and bent down to pick up the crow. His hands looked very white against the black of its feathers.

"It's warm," he said. "And it's got blood coming out of it."

"I think it's dead," I said. "We can bury it out here in the fields, if you like."

But even before I finished speaking Kenny's face exploded into a smile.

"No! I can feel it breathing!"

And then I saw too the gentle rise and fall of its chest.

"I'm taking it home. We can take care of it till it's better," Kenny said. "Like Snuffy."

Snuffy was a baby badger we'd found and looked after last year. I can't say exactly how, but that badger had sort of saved our family. My dad was falling apart, and Kenny was in a bad way about our mum, and everything seemed rubbish. But having the badger to take care of made us all better than we'd been before.

I looked at Kenny holding the crow, his face full of hope and love.

"Yeah," I said. "Good idea. Dad'll know what to do." Then I took my scarf off and wrapped it around the bird.

Close up, it didn't look black any more. The last of the sun gave its feathers a purple sheen, like petrol floating on a puddle. And at the place where the beak met the bird's face, the feathers were thin, and bare grey skin showed through.

"Look at this, Kenny," I said, and I pointed at the base of the beak. "It's sort of going bald, there. A bit like Dad's going bald on top of his head."

"Oh, yeah," Kenny said. "Does that mean he's like an old crow?"

"I don't think so. I think it isn't a crow at all. It's a rook. A young'un. They only get the white face when they grow up."

"So it's a baby?" Kenny said.

"Not really. More like a teenager. Like you and me."

That pleased Kenny.

"Yeah." He grinned. "Like us." And then his face went serious again. "He's not gonna die, is he? I don't want him to die ..."

"I think he'll be OK, Kenny," I said. But I didn't know.

Three

Kenny carried the rook home, like he was one of the Three Kings bringing presents for the baby Jesus. It lay in my scarf as if it were dead. Even Tina seemed to sense that something serious was happening, because instead of yapping and barking she trotted along beside us, not even stopping to sniff at the lamp-posts.

I had been shocked by how light the rook was, for such a big bird. I was going to say it was as light as a feather, but that doesn't mean anything. Even a little dog like Tina feels kind of solid and real, because of the meat and bone in her, but the rook felt like you were carrying a dream or a thought.

When we got home Dad was still asleep.

"We should put it in the shed," I said.

Kenny shook his head. "Nah, it's too cold. Maybe when the rook's better ..."

"Dad'll do his nut," I said.

But Kenny had already made up his mind.

"Have we got the same box we used to put Snuffy in?" he asked. Kenny liked it when things connected like that. It helped him to understand the world.

"I don't think so," I said. "But I'll get one like it."

I found a cardboard box under the stairs. Kenny put the rook in, still wrapped up in my scarf. It lay there, not moving, but it was looking at us with its black eyes.

"Do you think it needs some dinner?" Kenny said.

"Aye. And so do you. Why don't you go out in the garden and find some worms, and I'll make you beans on toast."

"OK," he said. "But don't put too much butter on the toast. I don't like it too buttery. I like it more beany."

So I made him some beans on toast, and it was ready when he came back.

"I could only find one worm," he said, "cos it's dark now."

What he held up wasn't a worm. It wa
worm.

"The rest of the worm got stuck in the grou
he said. "But that's OK, because Miss told us at
school that they can grow back when half of them
gets chopped off. So this is better. Rooky gets his
dinner, and the worm can grow a new back end."

"Rooky?" I said.

"Yeah, that's his name."

"It's a bit rubbish."

"Why?"

"Well, it's just what it is, a rook, with 'ee' on the
end. Sticking 'ee' on the end is the lamest name
ever."

"So what?" Kenny said. "That's what Rooky's
called. Anyway, I'm Ken with an 'ee' on the end,
and what's wrong with that?"

I didn't really have an answer to that.

While Kenny was eating his dinner, I tried to
get Rooky to do the same. The half-worm still had a
bit of wriggle left in it, which was pretty gross.

Rooky watched me from deep in the cardboard
box. For the first time I saw him move his head a
little. I held the worm just in front of his strong
grey beak. It opened a tiny bit.

came over, his mouth stained orange
. beans.

.e's gonna eat it!" he said.

But then Rooky closed his beak and his head
.umped back down into the scarf again.

I looked at Kenny and saw his eyes were wet.
Kenny had no filters. If he thought something, he
said it. If he felt something, it showed on his face.

"He'll be all right, Kenny," I said. "He just needs
a rest. And he's a bit bashed up, from that nasty
hawk. Dad might be able to fix him."

"What can Dad do?" a voice said from the
doorway. It was my dad, still bleary-eyed from his
kip. "Bloody hell, lads," he said, when he saw the
box on the kitchen table. "What's this then?"

I opened my mouth to tell him, but before I got a
word out, Kenny had explained the whole thing.

"This hawk was eating Rooky, but we saved
him, and now we're going to look after him till he's
better, and you can help, and Jenny, too."

Jenny's my dad's girlfriend. She's really nice,
and me and Kenny like her a lot.

"Let's have a look then," Dad said.

He picked up the rook, and held it gently in his
big hands. He stretched out one of the wings, and
the rook managed to peck at him.

"Ouch," Dad said, with a chuckle. "Stil
life in you yet."

And then the outside door opened and Jenr
came in, saying "Knock knock" out loud, which we
a thing she did. I reckon it was so we didn't think
she thought she owned the place. But she spent
quite a lot of time here. She worked as a nurse
at the hospital with Dad, and she drove him there
quite often, because we didn't have a car.

It was Jenny who cleaned out the cuts on
Rooky's back and breast. She used those little
sticks with a blob of cotton wool at the end, and
some TCP.

"I bet that stings," Kenny said.

"We should take him to the vet," said Jenny. "I
know about looking after humans, not birds."

"That'll be money ..." my dad said.

We all went quiet for a bit. We didn't have
much money. Not enough to spend on wild rooks.

"He'll be all right," Kenny said. "Me and our
Nicky'll look after him."

After that, Dad and Jenny went to work. Me and
Kenny stayed in the kitchen with Rooky. I think
Kenny thought that we could just sit there and send
waves of love, and that would keep the bird alive.

was in his box in the corner. We'd torn
the newspaper into strips so I could have my
back. The rook was still in a sort of a daze,
every now and then I heard the paper rustle
as he moved, so at least we knew he wasn't dead.
Kenny's love must have been working.

In the end even Kenny got tired of sitting and
staring, so we went off to bed. I made sure the
kitchen door was shut – Tina had been trying to
come in all night, and we knew what would happen
if she did, and it wouldn't be pretty.

Four

When I got up the next morning, Kenny was already out in the garden collecting worms for Rooky. He came into the kitchen, grinning.

"I've got two!" he announced, holding them up in his dirty fingers.

We crouched over Rooky's box. The bird was quiet and still, and I was sure he had died in the night. What could I say to Kenny? That he was in heaven? That it was the circle of life, like in *The Lion King*? The trouble was that Kenny was scared of losing things he loved, and of getting left behind. I felt sick inside, and I wished we'd never found Rooky.

But when I put my hand in the box, Rooky moved his head and tried to snap at me. It was a

.d feeble show of life, but life is what it was. hadn't given up, and nor would we.

Kenny dangled a worm in front of Rooky's beak. Rooky tilted his head on one side, and then he grabbed it. It was fast, and Kenny let out a squeal that was half joy and half fear. Rooky shook the worm a couple of times, then swallowed it down, and Kenny laughed.

"My go," I said, and the warmth of happiness and relief drove out the grey of sadness. "Give us that other worm."

"No way," Kenny said. "Finders keepers, losers weepers. You get your own."

Then he fed the other worm to Rooky.

I didn't fancy going out in the cold and scrabbling in the dirt.

"I reckon he'd like some Coco Pops," I said. "As a dessert after his worms."

I went and got some from the cupboard. I thought about holding my hand out flat, the way you feed a slice of bread to a horse, but I was worried about getting pecked, so I chucked them in the cardboard box. Rooky ignored them.

"He likes my worms better," said Kenny.

"He's probably just full," I said. "He'll ⬛
later. Anyway, now it's your turn to have so⬛
breakfast."

So I tipped Kenny and me out our Coco Pops,
and poured the milk over them.

Kenny munched away, and then a light came
into his eyes, as if he'd just remembered something.
I thought it was about Rooky. But it wasn't.

"I've got a secret," he said. "I was gonna not tell
you it yesterday, but I forgot. So now I'm gonna not
tell you it today."

"Oh, please, Kenny," I said. "Please tell me. I'll
die if you don't."

Now, the thing about Kenny is that he's the
worst secret-keeper in the history of the world.
If I'd just said "So what?" then he'd have told me
straight off. But that wouldn't have been fair, as I
knew he loved this game.

"No way!" he said. "It's too big, too ..." He
paused, searching for the right word. "Too *deadly*!"

"Oh, please!" I stretched the "please" out till it
was like "pleeeeeeeeeeaaaaaaaaaasssssssse".

Kenny shook his head. "No. I could kill you, but
then I'd have to tell you."

What he meant was, "I could tell you, but then
I'd have to kill you." He'd heard it on the telly and

of his favourite things to say. But he
ᵧot it muddled up. I didn't mind – I liked his
n.

"I'll give you a pound if you tell me," I said.

Kenny thought for a few seconds, then said,
"No."

I was impressed. It really was a big secret if I
couldn't buy it for a pound.

"I'll let you have my half-hour on the
PlayStation."

We were only allowed half an hour each per
day on the PlayStation. That was Jenny's rule.
Like I said, Jenny was dead nice, but she was strict.
She was against Coco Pops, too, but it was the only
thing Kenny would eat for breakfast, so she gave
in. You couldn't really complain about Jenny's
half-hour rule, as we only had a PlayStation
because she'd got it second-hand off the internet.

Kenny's thumbs twitched as he imagined
himself using the controller.

"OK. Right," he said. "I'll tell you. You know
that new kid at our school?"

I didn't really know who he meant, but I said,
"Yeah."

I thought Kenny's big secret was going to be that this kid could fart the alphabet or that he knew the right word for a girl's thingy.

"He's the Doctor from *Doctor Who*."

"What?" I said.

"Not What, Who. Doctor Who. He's Doctor Who."

I looked at Kenny. I had no idea what he was on about.

"Are you catching flies?" Kenny said. That was something our dad said when he left his gob hanging open, like mine was now. Then he sighed and tutted, as if I was being really dense, and repeated it.

"This boy, in my school, he's Doctor Who."

"Sure he is," I said.

Now I guessed that this was some joke he'd heard, and he was waiting to deliver the punchline. Then I remembered a rubbish Doctor Who joke, and I thought I'd tell Kenny before I forgot it again.

"What does Doctor Who eat with his pizza?"

Kenny looked puzzled.

"I don't know, but I can ask him."

"No, it's a joke," I said.

"What is?"

"What does Doctor Who eat with his pizza?"

Kenny still looked confused.

"I don't know," he said. "We haven't had pizza for school dinners since he came."

"Oh, I give up," I said, thinking the joke wasn't worth it. Then I remembered what we were talking about. "So how do you know this kid is Doctor Who?"

"Because he told me."

Kenny believed almost anything you told him. It's why I hated lying to him. There was no fun in it.

"Yeah, but, Kenny, people don't always tell the truth."

"Doctor Who does," Kenny said. "He never tells lies. So if this kid says he's Doctor Who, then that must be true."

"It dunt work like that, Kenny, he –"

"And anyway, he does magic."

"What?" I said.

"He can make money come out of your ear, and if he says pick a card, and you get one from anywhere in the pack, he always knows what it is. The Queen of Cubs, or the Joker or anything."

"Yeah, but –"

"And he knows everything. If you tell him your birthday, and how old you are, he can tell you what day you were born on, Monday, Tuesday, Friday, whatever."

"That's not –"

"And he can speak backwards, like if you tell him any word, he can say what it is backwards, so he calls me Eneck, like Y-N-N-E-K, instead of Kenny, and if he met you, he wouldn't call you Nicky, but ... well, I can't do it. But he says I can be his new assistant, because he needs one."

For the last bit I wasn't really listening, because I was trying to work out Nicky backwards.

"Eckin," I said.

"What?"

"Eckin. Y-K-C-I-N."

But Kenny wasn't interested.

"Anyway, so that proves it," he went on. "If he wasn't Doctor Who, he couldn't do backwards talk or know what day you were born on."

I was smiling a bit by now, and I didn't want to spoil it for Kenny, so I said, "OK, that's brilliant. I wish Doctor Who was my friend. But just be careful on your adventures."

And Kenny was happy with that.

"Your turn, now," he said.

Five

"Now I've told you a secret, you have to tell me one," Kenny said.

"That's not fair," I said. "I already said you could have my half-hour on the PlayStation."

"It's a rule. A secret for a secret. The PlayStation was on top of that."

"Why? That's stupid."

"It's a rule," Kenny said again. "To make it balance up. And it can't be a rubbish secret, like where Dad hides the Quality Street at Christmas, because I know that."

I saw Kenny's eyes light up with the colours of the sweet wrappers, gold and red and green.

"Really?" I said. "Where does he hide them?"

"If I tell you that you'll owe me two secrets. And you'd just eat them."

"The secrets?"

"Don't be stupid. The sweets."

Even when my dad was in a bad way, we always
had a giant tin of Quality Street at Christmas. It
was the best thing about it. One Christmas lunch
we just had some soup and oven chips, but
afterwards my dad got the tin of Quality Street
out, and we ate them all in front of the telly.

"I know what you're doing," Kenny said. "You're
trying to talk about something else, so you don't
have to tell me your secret."

"But what if I haven't got a secret?" I said,
looking up at the ceiling, then down at the floor.

"Hah!" Kenny said. "I know you've got one,
because you've been acting funny, and Dad and
Jenny said not to ask you about it."

I laughed. Sometimes I forget that even though
Kenny has learning difficulties he can read me like
a book. Better than a book, as his normal reading's
a bit slow, and he has to put his finger under every
word and spell it out. That's why he likes me to
read to him, otherwise the story goes too slow, like
when you're stuck in a traffic jam.

"OK then," I said. "My big secret is that I've
saved up £20, and I'm going to buy a new knock-off
Leeds United shirt from the market."

Kenny looked at me and his face was blank. With most people, when their face looks blank, it's because their brain is blank, but it was different with Kenny. His face went blank when he was doing his hardest thinking. It was as if all his brain power was being used up in the thinking, and there was nothing left over to be in charge of his face.

"That isn't your big secret," he said. "That's not a secret at all. It's just a ... a ... *thing*. To be a secret it has to be something you don't want people to know."

He'd got me.

"OK, then, my big secret is that I know how to fly."

Kenny gave me a look. "That's just a bloody big lie."

"Don't swear, Kenny," I said. "Not when you don't have to."

"Don't tell bloody great big lies, then."

He had a point. Kenny was definitely getting better at telling truth and lies apart. A few years ago he would have believed that I knew how to fly.

"OK, then," I said. "I know a special Kung Fu ninja move that makes me invisible. It's called the Silent but Deadly Dragon."

Kenny laughed.

"That's not a ninja move, it's a kind of fart. I'm not dumb."

"No, it's true!" I said.

"Go on then, do it!"

"OK, I will. But I've warned you, it can be very dangerous."

Kenny didn't really believe in the Silent but Deadly Dragon, but he still watched very carefully. I think he thought I was going to do some kind of trick, and he wanted to work it out.

"Come a bit nearer," I said.

He came forward a couple of steps.

"Are you paying attention?"

"Yes. I'll see if you cheat."

"Right," I said. "This needs all my brain power. It begins like this ..." I turned so my left side was pointing at Kenny. "Then I do this ..." I lifted my left arm up, bent at the elbow. "And now this." I lifted my left leg off the ground, with the knee bent.

Kenny's mouth fell open. He knew something amazing was about to happen. Something truly special. Something unique. And he was going to be there to witness it. I beckoned with the fingers of my left hand, and Kenny shuffled forward.

And then I hopped in the air and let rip with the massive fart I'd had brewing ever since Kenny came into the kitchen. The blast of it sent Kenny spinning away, and left me flat on my back, laughing so much I thought I was going to wet myself.

And the best thing is that Rooky answered with a *CRAAAAAK* of his own from inside his box. I don't know if he really was responding to the fart, or if he was going to caw anyway, but his timing was spot on. It tipped me and Kenny into hysteria, then Kenny jumped on top of me, and I couldn't fight him off because I was laughing too much.

Then I heard the door creak open and I looked up to see my dad laughing at us. But then his expression changed, and he flapped his hand in front of his nose.

"Bloody Nora," he said, choking. "Get them windows open. That's thick enough to dunk your bread in. It smells like a tramp crapped his pants and hid them in here. It's not human. It smells like a skunk farted. Worse, it smells like a cabbage and an egg got married and had some babies, and then they all died in here. No, not all of them, one grew up into a giant cabbage egg, and then *it* farted. No, worse, it's like someone farted, and it came alive in the form of a fart monster, and then that farted.

And now it's going to kill that poor bird, as if it hasn't suffered enough."

And each thing he said made me and Kenny laugh more.

And then Jenny was behind him, and she said, "Oh, God, that's singed my eyelashes off, that has. I'm not going in there without one of those suits they use for nuclear disasters."

And then Kenny said, "That was his bloody secret – he had a skunk living up his bum."

And that set us all off again.

Six

The weird thing was that Kenny was right.

I did have a secret, and it wasn't the Silent but Deadly Dragon.

I saw a thing on the telly once about this kind of wasp, which lays its egg inside a caterpillar. A tiny white maggot hatches out in the caterpillar's body, and it grows bigger and bigger and eats up the caterpillar's flesh until it fills up the whole of the inside of it, and then the caterpillar dies and the new wasp comes out. And while the caterpillar is alive it's just a slave of the wasp inside it, eating just so the wasp can be born.

My secret was a bit like that, inside me, taking up all the space, until it could come out.

Except that makes it sound gross, like a horror film, and this wasn't a horror film. Or not really, even if it did make me feel a bit sick, and a bit scared. But in a good way, if that makes sense.

It was a twenty-minute walk to my school. All the way there I could feel the secret inside me. It wasn't like the wasp-maggot today, but more like when you have a sweet in your mouth, and for as long as it's there you're happy, and its sweetness fills your whole gob up, and the only thing that stops it being perfect is that you know it won't last for ever.

I got to the back gate of the school. There were some kids hanging out there, same as always. I used to dread it, back in Year 7 and 8, but now I wasn't that bothered. There were still a few kids who said things about Kenny and about my mum, but it didn't upset me like it used to. I was stronger on the inside now.

Trouble is, sometimes you have to be stronger on the outside, too.

Three of the kids moved so they blocked the gate. They were from Year 10. Two of them were big and thick and scruffy. Shirts out, ties loose, even though the day had only just begun. Jenny

 35

always made me and Kenny go off to school looking neat, even if it didn't last.

One of the big lads had a tab between his knuckles, smoking it the way he'd seen the hard men do outside the pub.

The third kid was small and dark and neat. He had black eyes that didn't smile, even when the rest of him was laughing. His name was Pete Stanhope, but everyone called him Stanno.

"Hello, Nicholas," he said, sweet as you like. "How's your kid doing?" He meant Kenny.

"He's OK," I said, trying to find a way past them. But wherever I moved, they moved to block me.

"How's he getting on at his new school?"

Stanno was still being sarcastic. I think he was planning on keeping this up for a bit longer, but one of the apes with him sniggered, and then they all burst out laughing, and Stanno screamed, "SPECIAL SCHOOL, cos he's SPECIAL." Then the three of them started acting out like they were mental, making gormless noises and staggering around waving their hands in front of them.

I was about to push past them when a voice came from behind.

"Funny. Really funny. Think it'll be funny when I tell Mum and Dad about them websites you've been looking at."

I turned round. It was Sarah Stanhope, Stanno's sister. She was in my year. She looked like her brother. Same dark hair and eyes. Same small, neat mouth.

The two apes laughed even louder, but it froze Stanno solid. The smirk was off his face.

"You're talking shit," he said. "There's nothing ..."

"You should be more careful about deleting your history," Sarah said. Then she listed some websites. It was kind of funny, and kind of shocking to hear her say words like that. With each one the apes cheered and Stanno went redder. Then he called her some bad words, and the two apes stopped laughing.

Sarah pushed past the three of them and walked on into school. She hadn't said a word to me. I felt really embarrassed that she'd stuck up for me like that and I didn't know what to do. As I followed after her I thought I should say thanks, maybe make some kind of joke, but I knew I wouldn't have the guts.

Then I felt a stinging slap on the back of my head. I turned round to see Stanno there with his apes. Their faces were rigid with threat, like they were made out of rock or metal, not flesh.

"Say a word about this and you're dead," he said. "You and the spaz."

I thought then that I was going to lose control and punch Stanno so hard in the face he wouldn't have a face left. I didn't care if I got a beating off his thick mates. But then I looked behind him and saw the smiling face of Mrs Plenty. She was our Biology teacher and everyone liked her. Most of the teachers came in cars, but she got the bus, and so she came in this way.

"Come on now, Nicky," she said, in her friendly voice. "I bet you haven't done your Biology homework, have you? If you come with me, you can scribble some rubbish down before class. It won't be any worse than usual."

Then she swept past, and I followed her. I looked back over my shoulder. Stanno stared at me, pointed and mouthed "DEAD".

Seven

So there it is.

Sarah Stanhope.

Yeah, she was my secret, the real one. I fancied her so much my whole body ached, from my eyeballs to my toes. Every time I saw her it felt like my insides were boiling over, like when you leave the milk pan on the heat. I couldn't speak to her. In fact, I hadn't even tried. I knew I'd stammer and blush and talk rubbish. I couldn't even allow myself to look her in the eyes. She was out of my league – brainy, pretty, cool, popular.

The opposite of me.

And she was the sister of the kid I hated most in the school.

The rest of the day was weird. All the usual things happened, the lessons, the breaks, corridors

full of screaming kids, teachers shouting, *stuff*.
But all that was a sort of blur, like there was fog
all around me. All I could think about was Sarah,
and what I should have said when she stuck up
for me, or what I should have said after, or what
I should say to her now. I acted out scenes in my
head, but even in my daydreams I was useless and
tongue-tied.

I never used to be worried about how I looked –
clothes and hair and all that – but now all I could
think was how stupid my hair was, and that my
shoes were crap.

Part of me really wanted to talk about Sarah,
and part of me knew that I couldn't. I had two quite
good mates at school. There was Jonno, who was
a bit of a geek, but OK, and Ben, who was a bit of a
geek, but – well, you see the pattern. We weren't
exactly the coolest kids in school, but there were
some lower down than us on the food chain.

Ben – who we called Bendy, because he was
tall and bendy – was mainly into computers. Not
gaming or anything good like that, but designing
programmes and writing code. I didn't really know
what that meant.

Jonno was even less cool, because he had a sort
of obsession about the toilet. I mean, what he did in

there. He had all kinds of names for it, and he'd tell you in the morning about his toilet adventures. I suppose it's what can happen to you if you're 14 and haven't got a girlfriend, or the smallest chance of getting one.

Anyway, I couldn't talk to Jonno and Bendy about Sarah, because that's not what we talked about – we talked about computers and books and football and what sort of poo Jonno had done that morning. And if I told them I fancied Sarah, they'd look at me like I was mental, because it'd be like saying I fancied a mermaid, or someone famous off the telly.

So it was all inside me, with nowhere to go. And by 'it' I mean the feelings – the excitement, the fear, the confusion, the longing, the … well, I suppose I'm going to have to use the 'L' word, even though it's stupid.

Yeah, the love.

At least I didn't have any lessons with Sarah on a Monday. That might have killed me. It was bad enough seeing her across the school yard at break.

Eight

And then it was lunch time. School dinners were OK, as long as you avoided the 'healthy option'. It was always a baked potato with some kind of gunk. Sometimes the gunk was brown. Sometimes the gunk was yellow. There were usually chunks in the gunk, but always, the gunk was gunky. Yeah. Chunky and gunky, like something puked up by a monkey.

So I went for lasagne and chips. The lasagne came with the brown and the yellow chunky gunk. But it didn't matter. I wasn't hungry.

"Can I have your chips?" Jonno asked, when he saw I wasn't eating them.

"What? Oh, yeah."

"You definitely don't want em?"

"No. I mean, yeah, I don't want em. They're all yours."

Jonno reached over with his not-very-clean fingers to grab the chips off my plate. He made a mechanical noise and moved his arm in a jerky way, like it was a crane or a bulldozer with a grabber on the end. It was the sort of joke you'd make at junior school, and I felt embarrassed for him.

Then things got worse. While the Jonno-dozer was happening, I sensed some kids come up opposite us, with a clatter of plates and trays and cutlery. I looked up, thinking it'd be some other kids from my year.

It was.

Sort of.

Sarah Stanhope, and two of her friends.

I don't think Sarah had thought about where she was sitting, or who with. Then she raised her eyes, which met mine.

"*GGGGGGGGGGRRRRRRRRRRNNNNNNNN,*" Jonno went, and a few chips fell from his grabber.

"Crisis, crisis, crisis," he said, in a voice that was meant to sound like a walky-talky. "Send for emergency chip recovery squad. Over."

"Yes, sir!" he answered himself. "But there may be a delay. At present all our teams are dealing with a chicken nugget incident in the Alpha-Centauri quadrant. Over."

Then he bent down and ate the chips off the table, like a pig at a trough. As he did so, Bendy pushed the back of his head and squished his face into the chips.

"*Gettoff!*" Jonno yelped.

"Just helping you eat," Bendy said, giggling. "Yum yum, yum yum. Here, have some salt." He poured a load of salt over the back of Jonno's head.

This wasn't Bendy bullying Jonno or anything like that. If Bendy bullied you, it would be like someone attacking you with candy floss or balloons. They were just arsing about.

I looked at Sarah, and tried to make my face say, "Hey, I'm not with these bozos," but she and her friends had already begun to move away. Who wants to sit with some slobs who eat chips off the table and make bulldozer noises and pour salt on people's heads?

"Thanks, guys," I sighed.

"What?" Jonno said, when at last he was released by Bendy. His hair was all ruffled. There was a chip stuck to his face.

"Nothing."

Nine

It was stupid, really. Don't know what I was thinking. Maybe this is what happens to you when you fancy someone – you turn into an idiot.

I should have walked home with Bendy and Jonno.

And part of me really did want to get home so I could check up on Rooky.

But then I saw Sarah, by herself for once, heading towards the bus stop. All thoughts of Rooky went out of my head.

"I'm getting the bus into town," I said to the boys, and I scuttled towards the bus stop.

I think I had a sort of plan. To go up to her and say stuff. Like ... "I'm sorry about those two idiots ... And thanks for helping me out this morning ..." I don't know.

It was all really lame. But maybe when I opened my mouth poetry would pour out, and I'd tell her I loved her and wanted to get married and live in a little house in the woods or some junk like that.

There were loads of kids waiting for the bus, from Year 7 sprats to lumbering dinosaurs from Year 11. I'd seen Sarah get the number 15 before, and I just hoped it didn't come until I'd got up the courage to say whatever it was I was going to say.

I was standing by the shops, and Sarah was right by the bus stop. She had her earphones in, and you could tell she wasn't really in the street at all, but off wherever the music had taken her. I saw her lips move to the words of the song and I tried to work out what it was. My lips were moving as well, following hers, but I still couldn't tell what the song was. I was worried in case it was something terrible. She looked as cool as anything, but she could have dodgy taste in music. I don't think it would have put me off her. I think the only thing that would have put me off her was if she unzipped her skin and turned out to be half lizard.

And then I realised what I was going to say. I was just going to say "Thanks" and then she'd have to say "What for?" and then we'd be having a conversation.

A plan. It was a plan. It wasn't the world's greatest plan, but it was nice and simple, so even I couldn't mess it up. And I could tell her about Rooky, and ask if she wanted to come round and look at him.

I'd just got my legs moving, when the mob of kids all surged forward. It was the bus.

I could still have walked away, but somehow I couldn't. I moved with the crowd as it jostled, pushed and bumped, and next thing I knew I was on the bus. Most kids waved their bus passes at the driver. I didn't have a bus pass. I was going to buy a ticket, but I couldn't resist the crowd-surge, and I got swept onto the bus just in time to see Sarah disappear up the stairs.

It was too late now to go back. There were kids in between us, all fighting their way up the stairs.

And then I was up there, on the top deck. I saw Sarah. Amazingly, there was a seat next to her. She still hadn't seen me – she had her head buried in her school bag.

Was this it? Was this the chance I'd been waiting for? The chance to make a giant fool of myself. I hesitated. All I had to do was sit down.

And then someone shoved me from behind, and I was past her and in the back seats. The bus juddered into life, and it was chaos. Kids all laughing and yelling and swearing and throwing stuff. I was kind of relieved. If I'd sat next to her then I'd have had to talk. And as soon as I talked, she'd tell me to get stuffed, or she'd ignore me, look through me like I wasn't there, or look at me with disgust, like I was something stuck to her shoe.

No, at least while I was here, safe at the back, everything was still possible. I was on the cliff edge, but I hadn't jumped off.

Yeah, I'd just skulk here at the back till she got off, then get off and walk home. Lamer than a duck with one leg, but not total humiliation.

And then I heard the sound I dreaded most in the world.

Ten

"Tickets please."

Oh bloody hell.

The ticket inspector!

It was one of those sneaky ones who gets on wearing normal clothes to catch you out. He had one of those moustaches you only ever see on men who have a little bit of power, and who want to use it to cause the maximum amount of pain to everyone else.

This was a double disaster. If he caught me, it would mean a big fat fine. Even worse, Sarah would see it all, and the whole bus full of mad kids would laugh and jeer at me. I had to move fast.

The inspector moved up to the front of the bus. His back was to me. Sarah was staring out of the window, her head nodding slightly to her music.

I wasn't the only one who wanted to escape from the bus-ticket Nazi. As I got up and bolted for the stairs, half a dozen other kids did the same thing. I was first, and I made it just as the inspector turned round and yelled, "Hey, you!"

But by then we were all clattering down the stairs. The bus had stopped and an old lady was getting on. I didn't risk going for the doors in the middle of the bus where you're supposed to get off, and instead I ran for the front door. I was through it before anyone could stop me. The bus pulled away before the other kids made it.

Had Sarah seen me? The thought of it made me blush tomato red.

I suppose I should have got the bus back the other way, and given up on the whole stupid idea. But I wasn't in charge. I mean, the thinking part of me wasn't in charge. The bit of me that fancied Sarah Stanhope had taken over. It was nuts – like letting Kenny decide what we'd have for tea every night.

Anyway, I knew she couldn't live far away – there wasn't much of the town left – so I began to run after the bus. Two sets of lights, then a side street. There was lots of traffic, so it wasn't hard to keep up.

Three bus stops came and went. Each time
I waited, panting and praying that she'd get off.
Then, at last, I really would go and talk to her. I
even thought up another plan about what to say.
I'd say I'd seen her drop a pound, and I'd been
chasing after her to give it back. I know that plan
had more holes in it than my dad's socks but,
like I said, the clever part of me wasn't doing the
thinking.

Bus stop number four. At last I saw her coat
getting off the bus. With her inside it, I mean.
Obviously.

What to do? I couldn't talk to her now. I'd pant
hot breath all over her like a hand-dryer in the
public toilets.

So I followed her a bit more while I tried to
get my breath back. She still had her music on,
shutting out the world. She swung her bag in a way
you'd have to describe as ... beautiful.

Yeah, beautiful.

I could have watched her swinging that bag all
day. The lovely rhythm of it. Like a ... like a swing.
Yeah. She swung it like a swing. A beautiful swing.

At last my breath was under control. I was
about twenty metres behind her. Now. Just run up.
I got the pound coin ready.

I looked at it.

How could I pretend I'd followed her with the money? Was I going to say I ran after the bus all the way, like a dog chasing the postman's van?

I put the money back in my pocket.

No, I was just going to say, "Sarah, do you want to go out for a burger?" No, I bet she didn't eat burgers. Pizza, then. No, not pizzas either. What do girls like to eat? Nothing that got served with chips, that was for sure. Larks. Swan. No, not swan. That'd be like eating a dolphin or something. I had to make sure I never tried to get her to eat swan or dolphin. Maybe just a coffee. Yeah, that was safer. Not dolphin coffee, just coffee coffee. With a swan muffin.

I looked back up. She was gone. Disappeared into thin air. Like an angel. Wait, did angels disappear into thin air? Or was I thinking of fairies? I wished I'd gone to church more often so I'd learned about angels. But church wasn't much use for fairies. I didn't think there were any fairies in the Bible. Just on the Christmas tree. Or was that an angel?

I shook my head. I was going mad. Sarah hadn't disappeared, she'd just gone into one of the houses on the street.

They were normal houses. Bigger than the ones on our estate, but not that special. I was almost disappointed. Not that I thought she lived in a palace or anything. Or a fairy castle. But I thought her house would be more like something in an old book.

I walked down the street and looked at the houses, trying to work out where she'd gone. I suppose I must have looked a bit weird, walking along, staring at the houses like that. I also didn't want to be seen, so I was kind of scooting from lamp-post to lamp-post, like a crap spy or a secret agent.

And then I looked in one big front window, and saw a door open, and a black coat and a swinging bag enter, and Sarah flopped down on the sofa and reached for what I guessed must be the remote for the telly.

So I knew where she lived.

There was a white van parked a little bit down the road from her house. I went and hid behind it. No, not hid, just rested. Well, OK, maybe hid. Just while I did some thinking.

The coffee. That was it. I'd knock at the door. She'd open it.

"Oh, hi," I'd say. "I was wondering if you'd like to go for a coffee some time?"

"What, now?" she'd say.

"Why not?" I'd reply, like it wasn't a big deal, just something I did all the time.

"Yeah, cool, great."

But what if she asked how I knew where she lived?

I could say her friend must have told me.

But I didn't know any of her friends.

It didn't matter. I could cross that bridge when I got to it. I tried to check out my hair in the window in the back of the van, but the window was filthy. Someone had written CLEAN ME in the dirt.

I looked in the wing mirror. My hair was a mess. I smoothed it down. It sprang back up again.

That was the final straw. I realised that the whole thing was totally stupid. I felt a huge surge of hopelessness. Sarah Stanhope would never fancy me, would never go out with me, not even for a dolphin coffee. I might as well ask out an actual angel or fairy, not that they exist.

All I had to look forward to now was the long journey home. But in some ways I'd come out of it OK. It could have been much worse – at least she hadn't seen me.

I stepped out from behind the van, and bumped into someone coming the other way. He staggered back and I began to apologise.

Then I saw who it was.

His face was puzzled for a couple of seconds as he looked at me. Then it hardened, like cement.

"What are you doing here, you poof?" said Pete Stanhope.

Eleven

Until now, I had known where I stood with Pete
Stanhope. Him and his mates were the lions, and
me and my mates were the zebras and gazelles
running away from them. And that was sort of
rubbish, but at least we knew that they were the
predators and we were the prey. And that gives
you a bit of strength.

But now, here I was sneaking about outside his
house, spying on his sister. So now I felt weak and
wrong. It made me do something I hadn't done for
years. Stammer.

"N-n-n-nothing."

I used to stammer when I was a little kid.
I think it was to do with my mum leaving. I
remember being in Year 3 or 4, and trying to
answer a question and just getting stuck on

"Miss". "*M-m-m-m-m-m-m-m-m-m-m-m-m*" – it went on for ever, with all the kids laughing at me, and Miss Wentworth going from being patient to bored to annoyed. But I'd got over it. I don't know how. Sometimes bad things just go away all by themselves.

Until now.

"Well p-p-p-p-piss off then," Stanno jeered. He stepped close enough to shove me in the chest. I wasn't expecting it, so I staggered back, into the road. If there'd been any cars, I'd have been killed.

Sometimes I'd dreamed of a chance to get Stanno on his own so we could have a fair fight, without his meat-head mates to back him up. But now I was embarrassed, not angry, and I couldn't fight.

I picked myself up, planning to slink off like a whipped dog.

I thought he might close in to add a few kicks while I was down, but he was just staring at me. Then his eyes widened, and he smiled, and then the smile turned to a look of disgust.

"It's her, innit?" he said.

"What?"

"Our lass. You're ..."

"No!"

"You bloody are. You're, what is it … stalking her!"

"No!"

But my bright red cheeks gave me away.

"I can bloody see it," he said. "You creep. Trying to get a look at her, were you? Gonna sneak up to her bedroom window? You dirty pervert."

Then Stanno aimed a kick at me, and I covered my head with my arms while his trainers thudded into me.

Then, bored, he spat on me and walked away.

Twelve

It was dark when I got home. I'd started out pretty low, and by the time I opened the back door I felt like the blackness of the night had flooded into me, like water into a sinking ship.

The light of the house dazzled me. There was a smell of cooking, and I heard the telly from the front room. My dad was laughing at some comedy show. For years after my mum left, he never laughed, and now it seemed like he laughed all the time. It was as if the years of laughter had got stored up inside him, and now they were coming out.

But something mad inside me made me think that he was laughing at me.

"That you, Nicky lad?" he shouted. "Late for your tea."

"Well, you should have got me an effing phone," I snarled back. But I didn't say "effing" – I used the real word.

I didn't realise how angry I was about the phone until I opened my mouth. It was true that all my friends had mobiles except me. Dad said I could have one if I got a weekend job, but there wasn't any work around here, not even delivering newspapers. No one even got the papers any more, because of the internet.

I heard the silence from the other room. They must have turned the telly off.

Now my dad was at the kitchen door. He looked sort of blank. A blankness with anger in it. I'd seen it on the faces of men who were about to fight each other outside the pub.

It was because I'd sworn at him. I'd never done it before, not ever. I felt sick and I wanted to cry, but I was mad, too. Not mad at my dad really, but at everything else. It was just that my dad was in the way of it.

"We don't use that language in this house," he said.

"You used to swear all the time when you were drunk," I said. "It was 'shit this' and 'shit that'."

"Stop that, Nicky ..."

But, now I was going, nothing could stop me.

"And there was never any bloody food. Me and Kenny lived off toast for two years."

"I did me best."

"Well, your best was shit."

My dad stepped forward and drew his hand back, as if he was going to slap me. I didn't flinch. I'd done enough flinching. At that moment Tina appeared and started yapping, like she always did when anything kicked off.

"Go on, hit me, it's not like you haven't done it before," I said. "It's all part of being a shit dad."

But my dad didn't hit me. I don't really think he was going to. He hardly ever hit us, even when he was at his worst. But now Kenny was there beside him.

"Why's everyone shouting?" he said, looking from face to face. "Tina dunt like it. It makes her sad. And Rooky. He won't get better unless everyone's nice."

Rooky. I'd completely forgotten. I really wanted to know how he was. But if I asked about him, or even just went over to the box to look, I would have to back down. And I wasn't ready to do that.

"Shut up, Kenny," I said. "I don't care about that stupid bird."

And then I barged past them, Dad and Kenny, with Tina still yapping like a yapping machine. I went up to our room and slammed the door so hard the house shook. Then I threw myself on my bed and put my face in the pillow and lay there like a dead body. In fact, I wished I was a dead body, because dead bodies can't feel anything.

Thirteen

I share my room with Kenny, so I knew he'd show up in the end.

"Dad says you're a silly bugger, but not to mind as you've had a bad day," he said as he put his Spider-Man pyjamas on. He'd had them for ever, and they only came half way up his legs, but every time Dad tried to chuck them out Kenny got them back from the bin. I don't think he even liked Spider-Man. It was just the pyjamas.

I didn't say anything, so Kenny carried on.

"Rooky ate more worms, and he got better for a while, and he moved about in his box, but then he got poorly again, and Dad said he might have got germs in him and he should have medicine to kill the germs. Dad said if we waited you'd come down to get some dinner and play with Rooky, but you didn't."

"Shut up, Kenny," I said. "I'm trying to sleep."

I'd forgotten that I was hungry. But it was too late now.

"OK," Kenny said. "Tell me a story."

I used to read to Kenny a lot when we were little. Books from the library, because we didn't have any books in the house, except one about fishing, which my mum had given my dad for Christmas before she went away.

Kenny loved it when I read to him, but he liked it even more when I made stuff up. He called that a 'story by mouth'. I think what he liked about the story by mouth was that it could go on for ever, unlike a book, which comes to an end. He was always afraid that the book would be finished before he was ready.

"No," I said. "Just go to sleep."

"I can't unless you do me a story."

"Well, I'm not in the mood."

"If you don't do me a story, I'm going to do humming."

Kenny sometimes did a sort of tuneless humming which he said was to help him sleep, but I think he knew it was so irritating I'd give in and tell him a story. He was right, usually.

But, tonight, I was too annoyed and upset. If I told him a good story, he'd want me to go on for hours. So I thought my only chance of getting this crappy day over and done with was to tell him a really rubbish one.

"All right then," I said. "Be quiet and I'll get started."

Sometimes you can hear someone smile – a sound like someone carefully taking the wrapping off a present.

Then there was a scratching at the door. Kenny got out of bed and let Tina in. She always slept on his bed, even though that meant he had a dog's bum in his face all night.

"What's it called?" Kenny asked when he was back in bed with Tina settled next to him.

"It's called *Rook*."

"Is it about Rooky?"

"Sure. Maybe. Whatever. Right, so there was this rook. It was a young'un, not long out of the nest, so it knew sod all about staying alive. Then one day it got killed by a sparrowhawk. Because that's what happens in nature. The strong ones kill the weak ones, and then they eat them."

"That's not right!" Kenny said.

"Shut up."

"But it didn't eat him. Your story's wrong. Rooky's alive."

"Fine, then. This rook didn't get eaten straight away, because two stupid lads thought they could save it. So it lived for a couple of days, in pain, then it died and it went in the bin. And that proves you shouldn't mess with the law of nature, because you can't change it, and it would have been better for the rook if it had just died and been eaten by the sparrowhawk. The end."

I looked over at Kenny. His face was all screwed up, and he had his fingers in his ears.

I felt rotten. I'd never done this before – hurting Kenny, I mean. Hurting him on purpose. I hated myself. Maybe that's why I did it, to give myself a good reason to hate myself. I'd found a black cave of hate and crawled into it, like a ghoul from the churchyard, crawling into an old grave.

I lay awake until I heard Kenny's breathing become slow and regular. Then I heard my dad's heavy, weary tread on the stairs. And then I waited a while longer – I don't know how long, because time is weird when you're lying awake – and then I crept down to the kitchen and peered into Rooky's box. Kenny had put twigs and leaves and dried grass in there for him. I think he'd tried to make it look like a nest.

"Hey there, Rooky," I said.

The rook looked up at me, and I looked down at him. He was a mess. Feathers missing from his back and breast. I stroked him, and this time he didn't fight it. I scooped him up and sat on the kitchen floor with him on my lap. He stayed there, without struggling, the way a wild animal only would if it was dying. I didn't cry so much for the bird, as for me and Kenny and my dad. But yeah, I cried a bit for Rooky, too.

Fourteen

I hadn't shut the curtains, so the early morning light streamed in and woke me up. I was going to wake Kenny and say sorry, but then I thought it might be best not to mention the story. He was good at forgetting things, and if I reminded him about it, he'd only get upset all over again. I felt bad about my dad, too. I knew he was a nice man, a kind man, and now he'd got himself sorted out with Jenny, he was a good dad. But I still had too much rage inside me to say sorry.

But anger isn't all bad. There's a good part to anger. Anger is a kind of energy, and it makes you want to do stuff, not just curl up and die.

And I knew what I wanted to do.

Yesterday I'd been a pathetic loser. I'd followed Sarah around like a stray dog or a bad smell. A claggy fart. And then I'd let her brother boss me, even though he was on his own, without his mates.

Well, I was going to change that. Today would be different. I'd show Stanno, then I'd say sorry to Dad and Kenny, and everything would be OK.

I got dressed. Tina looked at me, and I thought she was going to beg me to feed her but then she snuggled back into Kenny's side. She was a thick dog, but not that thick.

I gulped some milk out of the carton, and grabbed the last crust from a sliced loaf to eat on my way. I got the early bus, and I was at school before any of the tossers were at the gates. In the playground there were just a few of the dweebs and nerds who always got there before the bell.

The yard started to fill up. A couple of kids said hello, but I just mumbled back.

And then I saw him.

Stanno.

He was coming in with his mates. He looked sort of pale, as if he was sick.

Good.

I hoped he was sick.

I was about to make him a lot sicker.

Here's what my plan was. I was going to face up to Stanno, right here, right now. I was going tell him he was a bully and a coward, and that without his meat-head mates he was nothing. Then I was going to hit him. One good straight punch, smack on the mouth, like in the movies. He would go down like a sack of hot shit. Then I was going to find Sarah and ask her out.

Good plan, I think you'll agree.

If you're an idiot.

I walked up to Stanno, full of a kind of jittery, nervous energy. It was like I had creepy crawlies running around on my skin, across my back and down my arms. I scratched and pulled at my clothes as I walked, like a dog with fleas.

Stanno's mates saw me before Stanno did. They looked at me, and they knew something was going to happen. One of them nudged Stanno, but he still looked distracted, like there was something else on his mind, something more important. And now it felt like the whole school was watching. Rather than the usual noise – the screams and yelps and laughter – there was silence.

At last Stanno seemed to notice what was happening. He looked at me, and tried to set his face hard, like his mates. But he still didn't look right. And that boosted my confidence. He was scared shitless. Scared of me. That had never happened before. He must have known that I was coming for him, and that he couldn't stop me.

I had hoped the right words would grow in my head and then come out of my mouth, like they do when a hero spits out a one-liner before he punches the bad guy.

But now here I was, right in front of Stanno, and there were no words in my head. But Stanno didn't have any either. He just looked at me, and his eyes were misty and out of focus. It was sort of embarrassing. His mates looked at him, and one nudged him again. He was supposed to lead them, let them know what they had to do. But he was standing there like a dummy.

So I had to do something. I didn't want to thump him, not before he said something to me, some wind-up. So I shoved him in the chest. I meant it to be a hard shove, hard enough to send him staggering back, like he'd done to me outside his house the night before. I thought that would set it all off. He'd burst back into life and have a go at me. Then I could hit him. Get it all over and done with. And maybe him and his mates would kick the crap out of me, but that didn't matter.

It wasn't a great shove. I was a bit too far away, and so my hands had already reached almost

...ar as they could go when they made contact ...th his chest. So it was the kind of shove you might get from a little kid. It shouldn't have done anything to him. He shouldn't even have taken a step back.

He didn't take a step back. What happened was that he fell over, like I'd hit him with a brick.

And then he was on his back, and his eyes were gone. White. You could just see the white. Then his arms and legs stretched out, then relaxed, then stretched again. And his back bent into an arch, and then straightened again. Then he started to shake.

I was too shocked to understand what was happening, though it should have been obvious. But I thought *I'd* done it, that he'd banged his head when he fell ...

Anyway, after a moment of silence, people were shouting.

"He's having a fit."

"Get a teacher!"

"Call 999!"

"You're meant to put them on their side so they don't swallow their tongue –"

"Or drown on their puke."

One of Stanno's mates came up to me, and he punched me, but I didn't feel it. It was only later that I remembered, when I looked in a mirror and saw that the side of my face looked like a plum. At the time I just stood over Stanno, not knowing where to go or what to do.

Then Sarah appeared. She looked at me, and there was so much hatred in her face that it burned me like acid. But she said nothing, and just kneeled down by Stanno's side and held his hand. She was the only person who didn't seem in a panic.

"It's all right," she said, and I'm not sure if it was to Stanno or the crowd of kids. "It's all right."

Then someone made a half-disgusted, half-laughing sort of noise and said, "Err, look, he's pissed his pants" And all the kids who were gathered round stepped back, as if Stanno was a bomb that was about to go off.

I couldn't stop myself. I looked and I saw a big dark stain spread down the front of Stanno's trousers.

Sarah took off her blazer and covered it up.

Then a teacher arrived. It was Mr Buck, who was a P.E. and Geography teacher, even though he was useless at all sport and couldn't find his own arse with a map.

"Stand back, stand back," he said, which
..ade all the kids who'd moved away gather in
a bit closer. "What's going on here? If you kids
are messing, there'll be ... what d'you call it ...
consequences."

"Sir, he's had a fit," someone said. "After *he*
pushed him."

A finger pointed at me. Faces turned. Mr
Buck's bulldog face was one of them.

"It's all right, sir," Sarah said. "It's epilepsy.
He'll be OK in a minute. I'll call my dad to take him
home."

I walked away, feeling like the worst person
who'd ever lived. Hitler, or someone like that.
Except Hitler didn't hate himself.

Fifteen

I got called into Ms Kemp's office before lunch. Ms Kemp is the Head. We don't normally see much of her, apart from Assembly on Wednesday mornings when she does a talk about the school's values, or personal hygiene, or being kind to each other, or how important it is to work hard and get good exams. But most of the time she stays in her room and doesn't bother anyone.

I'd been expecting it – getting called to her office, I mean. All morning people had been saying stuff like "You're for it, now," or "I wouldn't fancy being you." Jonno tried to joke about it, but Bendy shut him up with a look.

My dad was waiting in the corridor outside the office. He looked like a nervous school kid himself, as if he was going to get the cane, like they did in the olden days. There was a man and a woman there as well. The man had a suit on, and he looked like he'd rather be somewhere else. The woman had a furious face.

I guessed who they were – the man and the woman. Stanno's parents. Sarah's parents.

"Nicky, lad," my dad said, "what you been playing at?"

"Is this him? Is this him?" the woman said, and the pitch of her voice rose in anger.

The man put a hand on her arm. If he hadn't I think she might have got up and hit me.

But then Ms Kemp's door opened and she told us to come in and sit down.

"OK," she began, "thanks for coming in." She shook hands with everyone except me. "We're here because something very serious has happened. And I'd like to get to the bottom of it, before I decide what to do."

"There's no bottom to get to," the woman said. "This young thug knocked Peter to the ground, for no reason. Just belted him. And we all know what happened next."

I started to say something, but it stuck in my throat.

"I understand that Peter has epilepsy?" Ms Kemp said.

"He does, yes, it's in his records," said Stanno's dad.

Ms Kemp looked at some papers on her desk.

"But this is his first fit in school time?"

"He usually gets them at night," Stanno's mum said. "So that proves he was set off. Set off by this bully."

"We don't know that for sure –" Stanno's dad began.

"Look at him," Stanno's mum went on. "He's miles bigger than our Peter. Peter's only a little lad, he wouldn't hurt a fly. This animal ..."

My dad had been in a bit of a stupor up until now, but that made him wake up.

"Nicky's no animal," he said. "He's a good kid. He's never been in trouble."

"You," Stanno's mum said, her eyes red. "You, I blame you, the parents. You and his mother."

"Shut up," I said. "Shut your bloody stupid mouth."

There was a second of silence in the room. Then Ms Kemp said firmly, "Sit down, Nicholas, you're ..."

But it was too late. Something had blown in my head.

"You're all stupid. I didn't do a damn bloody thing."

"Nicky!" my dad said.

"Fuck off!" I said, more to the room than to him.

Then I ran out, slamming the door behind me.

I ran along the corridor, down the stairs and out of school.

Sixteen

Outside a fine rain was falling. It was the sort of rain that fills the air, even though you don't see the individual drops. I started walking home and soon I was soaked to the skin. I shivered. You're never truly cold unless you get wet.

I went along the back streets so my dad wouldn't see me on his way home. I thought he was going to be mad with me. He didn't know that I'd hardly touched Stanno. He probably believed that I'd bullied him. Adults never know what it's like, what really goes on in school.

Then I thought there was no point going the long way if I just ended up at home to get a bollocking. There was only one place I could think of to get out of the rain.

It took me half an hour to reach the library. My heart sank as soon as I saw it. It should have been all lit up, so you could see the books inside, and the people, and it would make you feel happy just seeing it. But it was dark, and I knew it was shut. I went up to it anyway.

There was a sign on the door. It said REVISED OPENING HOURS. It should have said REVISED SHUTTING HOURS, because it was shut nearly all the time. Now it was only open on Tuesday and Thursday mornings, and until 4 p.m. on Saturdays. It was mad. It was a nice building full of books, and now it was shut. It was like having a car you weren't allowed to take out of the garage.

There was a sort of porch over the door, which kept most of the rain off. I had nowhere else to go, so I slumped down on the step. I stayed there about an hour, getting colder and colder. When I couldn't stand it any more I got up. I checked in my pockets. I had two quid. I went to the chippy and got some chips and a Coke. I took them back to the steps and ate them. That made me feel a bit better. When you're eating, your thoughts sort of live in your mouth, with your food, and they don't float off to bad places.

But soon the chips were gone and then the goodness was gone too. Like when you're a tiny little kid and scared of the dark, and your mum comes and kisses you, and the force-field of the kiss lasts for a while, and keeps you safe, but then it thins, and thins. In the end it pops like a soap bubble and then they can get you again, the monsters.

So then I wandered around some more. The drizzle stopped, and I went up to the church, and into the graveyard, and looked across the field where we'd found Rooky, and beyond that to the little wood where we'd rescued the baby badger. But the rain came on harder again, and by now it was getting dark, so I went home.

Seventeen

I could tell my dad was waiting for me, because he wasn't doing anything else. Usually when you see people, they're doing things – watching the telly or mucking about on the internet, or reading the paper, or talking, or whatever. The only time you see people not doing anything, it means they're waiting for you. I suppose it's because people aren't great at multi-tasking, and just waiting is all they can manage.

And it also usually means you're in trouble.

Dad was sitting at the kitchen table. I got the feeling that he'd been thinking what to say for ages. He'd probably tried different versions – angry, confused, disgusted, annoyed, mocking. What was left was just sad.

"You shouldn't have done it, Nicky."

"What?" I said.

"Any of it. Hitting that kid. Effing and blinding. Storming out."

"I didn't hit him," I said.

"That's not what they said."

"I pushed him. Not even hard."

"Well, it was hard enough."

I thought about Stanno lying on the ground, shaking. I blinked to get the image out of my head.

"He was a bully," I said. "Not me."

"They all said he's smaller than you."

"Yeah, but he has big mates, and he always sets them on me. And he's ... sly."

My dad shook his head.

"Well, if you'd stayed and told all that to the Head, what's her name ...?"

"Ms Kemp."

"Aye, her. Well, maybe it wouldn't have happened."

It took a second for the penny to drop.

"What do you mean? What's happened?"

"You've been expelled."

"You mean suspended?" I'd guessed that was going to be my fate. "For how long?"

"Nicky, you don't get it. Not excluded, not suspended, but expelled. Kicked out. For good."

"No, but they can't –"

"Nicky, you hurt that kid, and then you said bad stuff to the Head. If you'd just said sorry, they'd have excluded you for a week or whatever. But you gave them the excuse they needed."

Something funny happened to my senses. Weird noises in my ears. My eyes stopped working and everything went blurry.

"Do you know what this means, Nicky?" my dad went on.

I looked at him and shook my head, not so much in answer to his question, but at everything, everything ...

"They have to find you somewhere else," he said. "Another school. And that means Milton Park."

Milton Park was the worst school for miles around. It was all boys, but not like Eton, or one of them posh schools. It was where all the bad lads went. The bad lads, the mad lads and the thick lads. No one went to Uni from there. From Milton Park you went on the dole or to jail.

And that was it, my future. I'd dreamed of going to Uni to study, I don't know, *something*. Poetry or science or the stars or history. And now I had lost it all, lost all that knowledge about the world, all the amazing things that were going to be in my head. I was going to be a junkie, a thief, a prisoner, and then dead.

"Oh, shit."

Then I saw that Jenny had appeared at the door.

"We can write them a letter, Nicky," she said. "A letter to the school. And another one to that boy's family. You can say sorry. They might let you off."

"They never let you off," my dad said. "They want to kick the bad lads out, to help them with the league tables."

"But Nicky's not a bad lad," Jenny said. "He just made a mistake ..."

I turned from one to the other. My dad looked defeated. Jenny looked like someone trying not to look defeated. That was worse. False hope is worse than no hope.

"What's the point?" I said, and I went upstairs.

It was only when I reached my room that I realised I hadn't seen the cardboard box.

That could only mean one thing.

Rooky was dead.

Eighteen

Kenny came into the bedroom later. I'd been lying there, staring at the ceiling. I'd got to know it quite well. It was made of that white stuff with a texture like the top of a trifle. I found that if I looked really hard at the ceiling, at all the little waves in it, at the cobwebs in the corners, at the dead flies stuck to the lightbulb, I could put off thinking about Milton Park, and how I was going to get the shit kicked out of me every day.

I was dreading talking to Kenny. I knew he'd be upset about Rooky, and I didn't think I had enough feelings left over for anyone else, once I'd finished feeling sorry for myself.

"Hey, our Nicky," Kenny said. He sounded pretty cheerful, like he always did, unless something had made him sad. He didn't have a middle – he was always one thing or the other. On or off.

I didn't answer him, but he went on anyway. I realised that Dad must have buried Rooky without telling him. Or maybe he'd told him Rooky had got better and flown away.

"Doctor Who and me are doing an adventure," Kenny said, as if nothing else mattered in the world.

"That's nice, Kenny."

"It's the day after tomorrow. You're invited."

I didn't know what he was on about. I didn't care, either.

"It's at our school," he went on. "Not in school time. In the night."

"Great."

I think Kenny realised then that something was wrong.

"Are you sad?" he asked.

"No."

"Good. Dad says come down for your dinner, now. Jenny made her special surprise pie."

Jenny's special surprise pie was a thing she did for Kenny. It wasn't really much of a surprise. It was either chicken, or fish, or beef, but she wouldn't tell you which, so you didn't know until you cut into it. Kenny's face was always full of excitement, and he always laughed when he found out what it was. You'd have thought there was a live kangaroo in there, not just some meat.

"I'm not hungry," I said.

Then I said something else. I don't know where it came from. Maybe I wanted to shake him out of his good mood, to make him see the world as it was.

"He's not Doctor Who," I said. "He's just some stupid kid."

"He is Doctor Who!" said Kenny. "You don't even know, because you haven't met him. You shouldn't say things that you don't know, cos saying stuff you don't know is lying."

"Doctor Who isn't real."

"You stupid bloody idiot, he is!" Kenny said, and he banged out of the room.

I lay there, still looking at the ceiling. A few minutes later the door opened. It was Kenny. I thought Dad had sent him back up to tell me again to come to dinner. But Kenny had something in his hand. It was one of his school exercise books. He threw it at me.

"I did the story about Rooky. The real story. Not the one you said. You did it all wrong."

Then he went out again.

I picked the book up and flicked through it. Kenny's writing was terrible, and his drawings were even worse. Then I found the last thing he had written in the book.

In the stori about Rooky who was a rook, my bruther Nicky got it rong becos he was sad wich make him forget wat hapen. Wat rely hapen was we saved him from the bad hork and then our dad took him to a place where they take care of porly things and make them better. Our dad said I coudlnt say good by to Rooky becos I was at school, but he wood let me see him after they let him go wen he was better.

So, that's what Dad had told him. I imagined my dad, in a few weeks, taking Kenny out into the fields and finding a flock of rooks. He would say one was Rooky, and Kenny would think he recognised him up there, a black fleck among hundreds like him.

Lies.

Everything was lies.

But sometimes you have to say things, even if you don't mean them, and you know they aren't true.

And sometimes you don't know what's true and what isn't.

But now I had something to do. Something to say.

Nineteen

No one noticed when I slipped out of the house.
Half an hour later I was outside Sarah's. It was
Sarah's house, but it wasn't Sarah I was after.

I was there to say sorry to Stanno. Sorry for
shoving him. Sorry for making him have that
fit. It was too late for it to make any difference
to anything, but that wasn't the point. You don't
do the right thing because it helps you. You do
it because it's the right thing. Well, no, that's
too simple. I was doing it to help myself, but in a
special way. I was doing it so I didn't have to feel
shit about not doing it any more.

But I was also doing it because of Kenny's story.
It made me realise that our lives are all about the
stories we tell. In fact, our lives are a story. And
it's up to you how you tell it. You can tell it sad, or

you can tell it happy. You can be a good guy or a bad guy.

I rang the doorbell. I'd always wanted to have a house with a doorbell. Something about the *ding-dong* cheered you up, gave you hope.

Stanno's mum opened the door. I'd been praying it would be Stanno himself. Or maybe his dad, who seemed OK.

It took her a couple of seconds to work out who I was, then she remembered, and almost snarled.

"You!" she said, and it felt like she'd hit me with a wet towel.

"I wanted ..."

She didn't let me get any further.

"Eff off," she said, and she shut the door in my face.

I stood there not knowing what to do. After a while I put out my finger and rang the bell again. The door opened straight away. Stanno's mum had a phone in her hand.

"You've got ten seconds, then I call the police."

"But I just wanted to ..."

"Eight seconds."

I leaned around her.

"Stanno," I yelled. "I'm sorry I pushed you. I'm sorry I made you sick. I'm sorry I did it."

"I'm calling them now," Stanno's mum said, and she pressed a button on the phone.

I didn't really think she was calling the police, but there was no point hanging around. I looked at her face. It was filled with hatred.

"I'm sorry to you, too," I said.

I admit, I didn't sound very sorry when I said it. It was more of a 'sod you' kind of voice. But I'd got the words out, and I did sort of mean them.

"Seven seconds ..."

As I turned away, I felt more defeated than ever. I just hoped this was the bottom. I didn't think I could take it if there was a level below this one.

Twenty

I started to walk back to the bus stop. I felt a bit better inside, the way you nearly always do when you say sorry for something. But that didn't help the fact that my life was about to turn to shit.

I'd reached the end of Stanno's road when I heard footsteps behind me. The way things were going, it couldn't be anything good. Either it was a mugger, or it was Stanno's mum, come to crack my skull open with a rolling pin. Or maybe it was Stanno himself, here to gloat. Could be all three, and they'd have a little party. But I didn't want to run. Running would add another layer of shame. So I hunched my shoulders and walked faster.

"Stop, you stupid idiot."

I knew the voice. It wasn't Stanno, or Stanno's mum.

I turned around and saw Sarah. She wc
wearing a big coat over the top of her pyjamc
even had her slippers on. They were in the shap
of bunny rabbits, with floppy ears. Her hair wasn
perfect now. It looked sort of ... tufty. I thought she
was coming to tell me what a jerk I was, and how
she hated me.

"It wasn't you," she said.

I didn't get what she meant. I must have looked
a bit gormless. She rolled her eyes like she was
talking to a simpleton. Maybe she was.

"Eh?"

"You. Peter."

"I ... I don't know what you mean."

She added some tutting to the eye-rolling.

"It wasn't you that made him have the fit. It
was coming on anyway. You can't make someone
have an epileptic fit by pushing them. Not a push
from a wimp like you, anyway."

At last it was sinking in. The way Stanno had
been looking weird. How easily he'd fallen down.

"But your mum ..." I began.

"She was upset," Sarah said. "He's her little
boy. And what with his epilepsy ... well, she's
wrapped him up in cotton wool."

. didn't know what to say. Part of me
a to scream that it wasn't fair, that my life
going to be ruined by this. But another part
anted to play it cool. And another part was
rizzing like a shaken-up bottle of Fanta, because
I was speaking to Sarah, and she'd run down the
street after me, wearing her bunny slippers.

"Look," she said, and her voice was softer,
less sarcastic. "I can't talk now. Can I meet you
tomorrow? There's things I want to tell you."

"I've been kicked out of school," I said.
"Expelled."

"Oh." Her face went blank. "I didn't know that.
You mean suspended?"

"No, for good. I'm going to Milton Park, with the
nutters."

She thought for a couple of seconds. I spent the
time thinking how beautiful she was, in her coat
and pyjamas and bunny slippers.

"OK, well, I can get out of school at lunch time.
See you in Starbucks at 12.30?"

"Er, OK. Not like I've got anything better to do."

And then she was gone, flickering in and out of
the orange pools of the street-lights.

I didn't know what had just happened, or what
it meant. But for that moment things didn't seem

quite as hopeless. I tried to remember that sa̶
the one about the darkest hour being the one
before dawn. But then I remembered there was
something called a false dawn, when you think the
sun is about to rise, but it isn't, and the night goes
on even darker than before.

There was no one up when I got in. But there was
a cheese and ham sandwich on a plate with cling
film over it, so it didn't dry up like a lizard's bum.
Cling film was a new thing in our house. It was
part of Dad getting his head together. There
was a note in Jenny's writing too –

*Put this in the sandwich toaster for three
minutes.*

Jenny was the main reason my dad got his head
together. Before her, we were a mess, but now we
were OK. Or we would have been if I hadn't screwed
everything up.

I didn't bother to toast the sandwich, but I had a
lump in my throat, which made it hard to swallow.

Twenty-One

When I went down the next morning, they were all at the kitchen table – Dad, Kenny, Jenny. I could tell they'd all been talking about me, because they shut up as soon as I came in.

Kenny broke the silence.

"Our dad and Jenny are going to find you a school that isn't as rubbish as Milton Park, where you won't get beaten up and called bad things and get your dinner money nicked."

"Cheers, Kenny," I said. I had forgotten that he didn't do sarcasm.

"Where did you go last night, Nicky?" Dad asked.

"Just out."

"We need to have a proper chat later," he said. "You know, make some decisions."

"Your GCSEs ..." Jenny said.

I nodded. But all I could think was – what point?

My dad said, "Jenny's going to look into other schools today. We might get you in somewhere that's not so bad –"

"Where you don't get your head kicked in," Kenny said, cheerful as ever.

"– Where you can still do the same GCSEs," Dad went on. "You never know, there might be somewhere."

"Thanks," I said. I looked at them, and they looked back at me. "I'm sorry I messed up."

Jenny put her hand over mine and gave it a squeeze.

That squeeze felt like when you've got a cat and it's sick and you take it to the vet, and they give it an injection to put it to sleep, and you cuddle it until it's dead.

They all put on their coats and stuff. Then Jenny said, "I nearly forgot. We've got something for you."

I didn't know what to expect.

"Don't get too excited," my dad said.

"IT'S A PHONE," Kenny said. "They said I couldn't tell you, but I can now, because it's time to give it you."

handed me the box. "It's only a nand pay-as-you-go. My sister got an ...de. We've put a tenner on it for you. Be ...eful with the data, or you'll use it all up."

I didn't know what to say.

"It's an iPhone 5," Kenny said, "but you can tell people it's a 5s, cos they look the same."

"It's great," I mumbled. And I hugged Jenny, and then my dad.

Then I hugged Kenny, and I said, "I'm sorry about Rooky. I know you loved the little feller. He's probably happier now."

"Yeah, I know," Kenny said. "He's better where he is."

And I thought it was good that Kenny was coming to terms with losing things.

Soon they'd all gone off, and I was left in the house on my own. Except, of course, for Tina. She'd always loved Kenny more than me, but now there was no one else in the house she decided that I was her best friend, and she came and sat on my knee while I mucked about with the new phone. It was pretty exciting. But then I realised that I didn't have anyone to call or message. So then I watched some crappy daytime telly. There was a chat show where women shouted at each other about who the

father of their baby was. Then some progra
where people tried to sell their rubbish old stu
Then another programme where people travelle
around trying to buy some rubbish old stuff. I
wondered why the two sets of people never met.
Maybe there'd be a massive explosion, like when
matter and anti-matter collide.

I fell into a kind of trance, with the telly on in
the background and Tina small and warm on my
lap. And it was all right. It was comfy. It was easy.

And then I thought that this was going to be the
rest of my life – watching daytime telly, waiting for
something to happen, moving from signing on for
benefits to signing on for my pension.

I might have stayed there on the sofa all day,
if Tina hadn't got up and scratched at the door to
be let out for a pee. I looked at the clock in the
kitchen. It was nearly half past eleven.

Bloody hell.

Sarah.

And I was still in the undies and T-shirt I'd slept
in.

I ran upstairs. I wanted to look nice. A couple
of years ago that wouldn't have been an option.
Back then my clothes were half in rags, and nothing
was very clean, because of the mess my dad was in.

...n't have much, but at least now it didn't
...or have holes in.

...found an OK shirt and an OK pair of jeans.
...he jeans were really Kenny's. He was taller than
me, but skinny, so they fitted OK round the waist,
but I had to roll them up at the bottom. I only had
the coat I wore for school, and I didn't want to wear
it, so I went out just like that, in a shirt and jeans,
even though it was cold out.

Oh yeah, there was one more thing. I kept it
in the shoe box under my bed, with other special
things. There was a broken penknife that I loved
when I was a little kid, running around pretending I
was Tarzan. There was a photo of my mum holding
me as a baby, and Kenny grinning at the camera,
and it was like he wasn't just grinning with his
mouth, or even his face, but with his whole body.
Other stuff like that. But also a watch. It was a
gold 'Rolex'. Fake, maybe. Real, maybe. Me and
Kenny found it in the Bacon Pond – the fishing lake
at the edge of town. It was as heavy as a tin of
soup, and the metal felt warm to the touch, almost
like it was alive. It had belonged to a dead man, but
now it was mine. I put it on.

Twenty-Two

I got there at 12.25. Five minutes to spare. I didn't know what to do. Should I wait at the counter until Sarah turned up, so I could get us both something? Or did I get myself a coffee, then wait for her at a table? And what was I supposed to order? I didn't really like coffee much, and I didn't have enough money to waste on it. I'd taken a tenner out of my jar. Thought I might have to buy Sarah a sandwich or something, as well as a drink. Would £10 be enough? I looked at the prices on the board behind the counter. But my eyes went blurry with panic. There were about twenty kinds of coffee.

"Can I help you?" a girl asked. She had a foreign accent, but I couldn't work out what it was. Not French or German. Just Foreign. She was kind

, and she smiled at me, which added to the
..

"I'm just, er, I'm meeting a friend. I mean
waiting for her. Till she gets here."

"She's here."

I looked around, sort of shocked, even though
I knew she was coming. She was closer than I
expected. I could have touched her if I'd bent my
head. Wait, hang on, that sounds like I wanted
to head-butt her, which was the last thing on my
mind. She wasn't in fluffy-mode, like the night
before, but in her school uniform. The uniform
made her look tough, like it was armour.

"Hiya," I said, and the word sounded stupid in
my mouth. Then I worried that it wasn't even a
word, just a sound I'd made up, or a noise you'd
yelp out while doing a karate chop. So I added, "Er,
hello, I mean."

Sarah looked at me like I was mad, and then
shrugged, as if she'd just decided to accept that I
was an idiot.

"Do you want anything?" I asked her. At least
that sentence came out in actual words.

"Mmmm ... Hot chocolate."

I wasn't expecting that. I thought she'd say "flat white" or "espresso" or some other cool kind of coffee I hadn't even heard of.

"Why don't you grab a seat," I said. "I'll bring it over." I really just wanted a few seconds to get my head together.

She nodded and found an empty seat in the corner.

I'd been putting off thinking what this was all about, but now my brain went into hyperdrive. Part of me hoped it was because she, er, sort of liked me. You know, fancied. But the sane bit of me knew that couldn't be true. The only non-mad idea I had was that she felt a bit rubbish about how I'd been dumped out of school. Yeah, she was taking pity on me. I wasn't sure how I felt about that, but I supposed it was better than nothing. At least it meant I had the chance to work my magic on her. If I had any magic.

I suddenly thought about Kenny and his friend, Doctor Who, and his magic tricks. And I felt a big wave of love for my brother rise up from my stomach, and with it came a jumbled-together urge to laugh and cry and dance all at the same time.

"What are you grinning about?" Sarah said, as I put her hot chocolate down in front of her.

And then I started talking. Talking like I'd never talked to anyone. I talked about Kenny. And I talked about my dad. And I talked about my mum. And then I did something even weirder. I talked about me.

Twenty-Three

I'd spent my whole life not talking about the things inside me, and now I'd spilled them all over the table, all over her, this girl that I didn't even know.

I'd have stopped if it hadn't been for Sarah's face. I mean, if she'd looked bored or annoyed or whatever. But she just listened, and nodded, and a couple of times she looked like she was going to ask me something, but then she didn't.

And now I was really embarrassed.

"I'm sorry," I said. "I don't know where all that came from ..."

"It's all right," she said, and she took the first sip from her hot chocolate. It must have been cold by now. It left a creamy moustache on her top lip. She must have seen me looking at it, because she laughed and wiped it off with a napkin. That sort of changed the mood and for a while we chatted about school and stuff.

And then at the same moment, we both remembered I'd been kicked out. But the memory seemed to have opposite effects on us. I tried hard not to be sad, but I felt my face begin to melt like an ice cream on a hot day. But Sarah seemed to cheer up, as if it was a happy thought. So maybe this was it. The whole thing was a wind-up. She was going to laugh in my face, and then laugh behind my back with all her mates. "Yeah, I really had him going," she'd say. "He thought I actually liked him. Loser."

"You don't have to worry," she said to me, now, not to her mates, later.

"Easy for you to say. You're not going to Milton Park."

"Nor are you."

"Pardon?"

"I had a long talk with Pete."

I groaned at the very sound of his name.

"He's not as bad as you think," Sarah said.

"I don't think you know what he's like."

"I think I know my brother better than you do," she said.

"You only see part of him ..."

"OK, right," she said. "I'm going to tell you something about Pete, and it's a big secret, and you must never tell anyone else. Got that?"

"Sure."

"OK, Pete's had epilepsy since he was a little kid. He gets different types of fits. He gets fits where he sort of stares, like he's kind of out of it for a while. And then he has big fits, like the one at school. He's on really strong medication to control it, and he's lucky he's never had any of the big fits at school. Well, not until now."

"Oh," I said. "I'm ... I didn't know."

She shook her head. "But the point is ... the point is how it made him act. Because he was basically bricking it the whole time. He thought if he had a fit at school, then everyone would turn on him. And that made him act tough. It made him play up to those idiots he hangs out with. He was just ... scared. Bricking it."

I thought about Stanno and how he'd behaved. Yeah, it made sense now. I could see how that would happen. But it didn't excuse everything.

"He called my brother names," I said. "Kenny, the one I told you about. He got strangled by his cord thing when he was born. He has special needs."

Sarah nodded. "I'm not saying he's not a jerk, my brother, but it comes out of him being scared. He's scared he'll get treated the same as Kenny. But part of him knows better. And the better part of him is winning now."

"Says you," I said.

"Yeah, says me. But he is doing something about it."

"Like what?"

"He told my mum and dad that it wasn't your fault," she said. "That he had the fit."

"What?"

"And my dad called the school this morning. He texted me about it. He told them that they had to let you back in. He told them that it was as much Pete's fault as yours. That you're not a bully. That you couldn't know he was about to have a fit. He said the Head told him they'd still have to suspend you for three days for fighting and swearing, but you could go back to school on Monday."

I couldn't believe what I was hearing.

"Is this some kind of ... joke?" I said.

Sarah pretended to be offended. "If I make a joke, you'll know, cos you'll be laughing," she said.

"So it's real ...?"

"The only thing not real round here is that eBay Rolex of yours," she said. "You should wear it with Mr Osmani's wig and Ms Kemp's false teeth. You could make Frankenstein's monster out of it all." Then she did a really rubbish Frankenstein impression, which was more a sort of general zombie.

That's when I knew she liked me.

You might think that's a weird leap. I don't suppose the websites and magazines that give you dating advice say that you can tell someone fancies you because they do a zombie impression. But I knew.

And then I started to laugh. Partly at the stupid zombie. Partly at the fact that my life might not be about to turn to total crap. Partly because the laughter was just there, inside me, and had to come out. It was the first time I'd properly laughed since the fart thing, and in the end I was laughing so much that tears were rolling down my face.

"It wasn't that funny," Sarah said.

But then she got the giggles, too. There's something about laughing together like that, that makes you ... close. It dissolves the barriers between you. There's just the real you and the real other person, touching, even if there's a whole table in between you.

Twenty-Four

Soon – too soon – Sarah had to go. "No point us both being suspended," she said.

"Can I have your mobile number?" I asked. I tried to sound confident, as if it was the sort of thing I did all the time.

"Course." She told it to me, while I put it in the address book on my phone. I must have looked like what I was – the only person in the world under sixty who'd never had a phone before.

Then it was done, and she was gone, and I watched her walk away, and I let out a sigh that jumbled together admiration for how cute she looked with relief that I hadn't totally screwed up.

But I still had the day to kill. I was thinking about getting the bus into town, but then I heard a cackle from a tree, and looked up and saw a magpie there. I knew magpies were in the crow family, along with rooks. It made me think of Kenny and Rooky. So I decided to go and meet him at his school.

When Kenny first went to his school, me or my dad had to take him and collect him, and he used to hate that. He was very proud when he was allowed to go on his own. It's a special school for kids with learning difficulties, some quite bad, some not so bad, like Kenny. Kenny loved it because he could do things that some of the other kids couldn't, and it made him feel good to be able to help them. So when we collected him from school it embarrassed and annoyed him. It made him feel helpless, like he wasn't in charge of himself.

His school finished at three, and I was at the gates when the bell went. It took a while for the kids to come streaming out. There were plenty of parents there, as well as some school minibuses. Kenny could have got one of the minibuses, and been dropped right at our door, but he liked to get the 'proper bus' not the 'special bus'.

The kids were all the usual shapes and sizes, but quite a few of them couldn't move too well. Some looked like they were trying to walk into a strong wind, and some looked like they'd been running really fast, and now they were trying really hard to slow down. A few were in electric wheelchairs. But that didn't stop them from mucking about. They looked just as happy to be getting out of school as every other kid in the history of the universe.

Then I saw Kenny. He was with a kid who only came up to his shoulder. The other kid was wearing a big coat that hung down below his knees. He walked along staring at the ground, as if he'd dropped all his money. There was only one person he could be – Doctor Who. Kenny was chatting and laughing, the way he does, waving his arms around like he was being attacked by killer butterflies.

Then he saw me, and his face changed. He started to look around, to see if anyone had noticed. Then he waved at me to go away. When I didn't move he glared and showed his teeth, like Tina when you took her bone away.

But I wasn't going anywhere. I waited for Kenny and the Doctor to come out the gates. Kenny came up to me and hissed, "You're showing me up. I go home on the proper bus by myself."

So, that was it. I'd embarrassed Kenny. It was kind of funny.

"I know, our Kenny," I said, "but I wanted to hang out with you, and I thought you wouldn't mind keeping me company on the way home."

It was always a good idea to appeal to Kenny's kind side.

"Oh, yeah," he said. "I forgot you was chucked out of your school. If you're still sad, you can come with me. I'm not bothered."

All the time the Doctor had been standing there, looking at the ground for his lost money, his hands deep in his pockets.

"Are you going to introduce me to your friend?" I said to Kenny.

"No," Kenny said. "He dunt like talking to people. He's having big thoughts inside his head. And he's planning his next move."

"OK," I said.

"We've got a mission," Kenny went on. "He has to think it all out."

"Nice."

"It's tomorrow night. In front of everyone. I told you about it."

"Great." I had no idea what Kenny was on about, but then I remembered he'd said something about an adventure after school.

"Oh, is it like a show or something?" I asked.

Then the Doctor rummaged around in one of his big pockets, pulled out a crumpled piece of paper and shoved it at me without a word. It was a flyer. And, yes, it was for a school show. A list of various acts. People singing or playing the violin. And then, at the end, 'The Great Doctor Who Adventure'.

"Dad and Jenny are coming," Kenny said.

"Me too," I said. "Can I bring a friend?"

"If there's tickets left. They cost two pounds. All the money goes to Africa for poor children."

"Does the Doctor get the bus with you?" I asked. Kenny shook his head. "No."

"OK. Shall we get going, then?"

"Go and stand over there and wait for me," Kenny said, and he waved me away towards the bus stop. When I got there I looked back and saw Kenny whispering into the Doctor's ear. Then, to my amazement, Kenny gave the kid a big hug.

It gave me a funny feeling. I suppose I'd always thought of Kenny as this person who only really existed when I was with him. There's that thing people say, about a tree falling in the desert. If nobody's there to hear it, does it make a sound? It's a bit stupid. You don't get trees in deserts. But that was sort of what I thought about Kenny. If I wasn't there to watch him, his life didn't exist. But now I saw that I was wrong. Kenny existed all by himself. He didn't belong to me.

The bus came and we sat upstairs at the front. When we were little, Kenny used to pretend he was driving the bus, and he'd turn his invisible steering wheel, and make bus noises. He hadn't done that for a long time, not so you could see him. But I could tell he was still doing it on the inside.

"Are you still sad, our Nicky?" he asked, while we were stuck in some traffic and he didn't have any driving to do. "Cos you don't look sad, and I thought you would be. Is it cos you've got a holiday before you start at that new bad school?"

"No, Kenny," I said. "I mean, you're right, I'm not sad any more. But not because I've got a holiday. It's because I don't think they're going to kick me out of my other school."

"That's nice," Kenny said.

And then the traffic cleared, and he had to focus on the important business of driving the bus back home.

Twenty-Five

So the next evening we were all there, sitting on hard plastic chairs in the hall of Kenny's school. Me, my dad, Jenny. And Sarah Stanhope. Sarah had sounded a bit uncertain when I'd called her and asked her to come, but whether it was guilt or something else, she said yes. Of course my dad and Jenny liked her before they even met her, because of how she'd saved me from Milton Park.

Some of the acts were pretty terrible. But some of them were OK, and when you looked around you could see the pride shining in the eyes of the mums and dads, and that made it kind of sweet. The teachers left the whole thing up to the kids, so there were a few moments of chaos, like when two acts both thought it was their turn, and a boy tried to sing one song while a girl played a different one on the violin.

Then it was Kenny's turn. A curly-haired boy with Down's syndrome came on stage like a circus ringmaster and said, "And now for our Doctor Who Magic Adventure."

Kenny and Doctor Who came out on stage. Doctor Who didn't seem so shy when he was on stage, but it was still Kenny who did all the talking.

He said, "The Doctor will now do magic with cards," while Doctor Who fanned open the pack and did various tricks with the cards, tapping them with his sonic screwdriver.

Then Kenny asked for a volunteer, and one of the mums came up and had to pick a card. Then Doctor Who tore it into bits, and Kenny swallowed the pieces, and then Doctor Who produced the same card from behind the mum's ear and everyone gasped and clapped.

Then Kenny announced, "For the grand finale, Doctor Who is going to transport into the future, because he can."

And then some kids pushed a cardboard model of the Tardis onto the stage, and Doctor Who got into it, and Kenny closed the door.

"Have you transported yet?" he shouted at the Tardis, and when there was no answer he opened up the door, and the Tardis was empty.

The audience gasped again, and Kenny's grin was as wide as the Grand Canyon. His whole body was smiling.

He shut the doors again and said, "Doctor Who is travelling to the future. He'll get there in ten seconds."

Then he got the audience to count down from ten with him, and he opened the door, and there was Doctor Who. He jumped out of the Tardis with his long coat flying behind him, and the two of them bowed at the front of the stage, while everyone cheered and clapped.

I looked over at Sarah, and she was smiling and clapping, and then she looked back at me and did a different kind of smile.

Twenty-Six

On Saturday morning my dad woke us up early.

"Get your kit on," he said. "We've a long drive."

Jenny made us breakfast. Porridge. I hate porridge, even when she tries to make it nice, with raisins and brown sugar. It still tastes like donkey sick, to me.

"Where we off to, Dad?" I asked, rubbing the sleep from my eyes.

"Outside Wakefield. That's where he is. Jenny's driving. It'll take about 45 minutes."

It was a refuge for wild birds. There was a visitor centre, and big cages, with owls and falcons and hawks.

"There's a bloody sparrowhawk," Kenny said, as we came to one cage. Inside was a sparrowhawk, dark grey on his back, reddy-brown at the front, with darker bars across his breast.

"Beautiful," Jenny said, and he was. "And mind your language, young man."

We went back to the visitor centre and my dad spoke to the lady on Reception, and we got shown in.

There was a bald man there, and he shook my dad's hand.

"Hello again," he said. "Back to check up on that rook, are you?"

Then we went into another room, which smelled like a doctor's surgery, and there were small cages, some empty, and some with injured birds.

And there was Rooky. He hopped up to the front of his cage and put his head on one side, staring at us.

"He knows you, Kenny," I said.

"Hello, Rooky," Kenny said. "You can teach em to talk, you know. I read it on the internet. They're dead brainy, like monkeys."

"*Craaaark*," said Rooky.

He was still shabby, with bare patches where his grey skin showed through. But I knew that rooks are always scruffy, compared to other crows, always in need of a brush-up.

"Is he nearly better?" Kenny asked the man.

"The vet says he needs a couple more days in here, just to make sure we've got the infection cleared up. Then a week out in the fresh air cages, and then we can let him go. Come back then, and you can see him fly off."

While Kenny was talking to Rooky, I said to my dad, "I thought he was dead. Dead and buried."

"Did you?" My dad looked at me. "You should have a bit more faith, lad. Mind you, I had to give them a decent donation to take him. To begin with, they said rooks were too common to bother much with. Too common and too scruffy and too much trouble. Bit like us, eh?"

I gave my dad a hug. And Jenny put her arm round me. And then I went and stood next to Kenny, and together we tried to teach Rooky some rude words.

Acknowledgements

My thanks to Emma Hargrave and
Mairi Kidd for their patience and editorial grace,
and to Jane Walker for everything else. Also, a
special thanks to Carolyn Soutar, whose kind gift
of a laptop meant that I didn't have to carve the
text with a chisel on stone tablets or whittle it
into trees or write it on my arm with a
quill pen and squid ink.

Our books are tested for children and young people by
children and young people. Thanks to everyone who
consulted on a manuscript for their time and effort in
helping us to make our books better for our readers.